ISABELLE B
Illustrated by Lu

The Billy Goats Gruff

Methuen Children's Books

Once upon a time there were three billy goats. The first was called Gruff, the second was called Gruff and the third, the biggest, was called Gruff too!

One day, they set off into the mountains to look for some fresh green grass to eat.

On their way, they had to cross over a bridge. But under this bridge lived an ugly old wolf. His great big eyes glowed like coal; his teeth were at least an inch long;

and his silver-grey fur was bald in places.
Wolf sat there, waiting for his next victim.

The baby billy goat Gruff was the first to cross, TRIP, TRAP, TRIP, TRAP over the rickety-rackety bridge.

'Who goes TRIP, TRAP, TRIP, TRAP over my rickety-rackety bridge?' called Wolf.

'It is I, Baby Gruff. I'm going into the mountains to look for some fresh green grass to eat,' replied the little goat, in a thin, piping voice.

'And *I* am going to eat you up,' said Wolf.

'No, no. I beg you, spare my life. Wait just a while — another billy goat Gruff is coming just behind me and he is fatter than me.'

'Well . . . all right. But run along quickly now,' replied Wolf.

A few moments later, the second billy goat Gruff arrived, **TRIP, TRAP, TRIP, TRAP** over the rickety-rackety bridge.

'Who goes **TRIP, TRAP, TRIP, TRAP** over my rickety-rackety bridge?' called Wolf.

'It is I, billy goat Gruff. I'm going into the mountains to look for some fresh green grass to eat,' replied the goat in a slightly less thin, piping voice than the first billy goat.

'How dare you go **TRIP, TRAP, TRIP, TRAP** over my rickety-rackety bridge? On my honour as a wolf, I shall eat you up straight away!' growled Wolf.

'No, no, spare my life. Wait just a while — the big billy goat Gruff is coming just behind me, and he is much bigger and much fatter than me!'

'Oh, very well. But run along quickly now,' agreed Wolf.

And the second billy goat Gruff continued safely into the mountains.

Then the big billy goat Gruff appeared, **TRIP, TRAP, TRIP, TRAP** over the rickety-rackety bridge. He was so heavy that the bridge creaked and shook under his hooves.

'Who goes **TRIP, TRAP, TRIP, TRAP** over my rickety-rackety bridge,' called Wolf.

'It is I, the Big Billy Goat Gruff!' said the goat in a strong, loud voice.

‘Ah,ha! Here you are.
One mouthful and you’ll be gone!’
‘Go on, then,’ replied
the goat. ‘See if you can!’

Wolf pounced.

But the big billy goat butted him
with his horns and killed him.

The three billy goats Gruff
were happy in the mountains.

They stayed there all summer.

By the time they returned to the valley
in Autumn, they were big and fat.